Desser
the Best
Ever Cat

Desser the Best Ever Cat

MAGGIE SMITH

Dell Dragonfly Books New York

𝒯his is a story about
the best cat who ever lived.
His name was Desser.

A long, long time ago, when my daddy had big hair, a teeny tiny kitten came to his door one day.

Daddy tried to find out where the kitten had come from.

Nobody knew.

So he decided to keep it. He named it Dexter after his favorite uncle. Then he made a soft bed and bought lots of toys.

But Desser's favorite game was to zoom through the rooms...

...and right up Daddy's leg!

Desser grew up fast.

Daddy met my mommy,
and they got married.

Desser liked his new house.

But Mommy says he was lonely.

Until I came along!
When I first came home
from the hospital, Desser
wasn't sure if he liked me.

But soon he got used to me. He sniffed me a lot and followed me from room to room.

He watched over me while I slept.

When I first started talking, I couldn't say, "Dexter."
But Desser didn't mind. He liked his new name.

He wasn't too happy when I first started walking,

but he was glad when I got my big bed.

When my parents were busy with my new brother Frankie, I always had Desser to play with.

In the morning, he'd sit on me and meow until I opened my eyes.

Then we'd
decide
what to do.

If Desser got bored,
he'd hang on a chair back
or stare at the wall.

Sometimes he'd do something bad.

But I could never stay mad at him for long.

When I started school, Desser was mad at me.
He would walk away with his tail up high,
like he didn't care I was leaving.

But he'd always be waiting for me when I got home.

Desser was always there.

As I got bigger, Desser slowed down a lot. He went blind in one eye, and he didn't want to do much. Sometimes his hair came out in tufts.

Then he got really sick. The doctor gave him some medicine. But she said there wasn't much we could do. Desser was old. Soon he could barely move, and he wouldn't eat anything. Not even for me.

"Is he going to die?"
I asked Mommy.

I didn't want him to leave me.

"He won't *ever* leave you," Mom told me.
"Because you will always, always remember him."

Dad got Desser his old bed, and I gave him my blankie
to sleep on. I lay next to him and patted him gently.
"You are the best cat," I whispered, "that ever, ever lived."
He opened his good eye and purred softly.

When I woke up in the morning, I was in my bed.

Desser was gone.

He had died in the night.

We buried Desser out by his favorite tree,
with most of his toys and plenty of treats
for the long journey up to Cat Heaven.

A month after Desser died, we went to the pound.
Dad said Desser would want us to get a new kitten,
because we are "cat people," especially me.
A little orange fluffball kept playing with my
shoelace. So I chose her.

I still miss Desser, but Ginger is lots of fun. She zooms around the house, just like Desser did when he was a kitten.

She also likes to sit on my shoulder.
I think Ginger is extra-special, and I'm sure Desser would agree. I show her his picture and tell her stories about him.

So she'll know about
Desser,
the Best Ever Cat.

To all the beloved
who have left us
for Cat Heaven

Published by
Dell Dragonfly Books
an imprint of
Random House Children's Books
a division of Random House, Inc.
1540 Broadway
New York, New York 10036

Visit us on the Web! www.randomhouse.com/kids
Educators and librarians, for a variety of teaching tools, visit us at www.randomhouse.com/teachers

Library of Congress Cataloging-in-Publication Data
Smith, Maggie, 1965-
Desser the best ever cat / by Maggie Smith
p.   cm.
Summary: A child describes how Desser the cat had always been part of the family and how much he was loved even after he died.
ISBN: 0-375-81056-0 (trade)
0-375-91056-5 (lib. bdg.)
0-440-41774-0 (pbk.)
[1. Cats—Fiction. 2. Death—Fiction.]   I. Title.
PZ7.S65474 Dh 2001
[E]—dc21   00-025441

Reprinted by arrangement with Alfred A. Knopf

Printed in the United States of America

April 2003

10 9 8 7 6 5 4 3 2 1